A Just Right Book

LAURENT DE BRUNHOFF

BABAR'S
BUSY YEAR

Random House 🏠 New York

Copyright © 1989 by Laurent de Brunhoff. All rights reserved under International
and Pan-American Copyright Conventions. Published in the United States by Random House, Inc., New York,
and simultaneously in Canada by Random House of Canada Limited, Toronto.
Library of Congress Cataloging-in-Publication Data:
Brunhoff, Laurent de, 1925– Babar's busy year : a book about seasons / by Laurent de Brunhoff. p. cm.–(A Just right book)
SUMMARY: The changing seasons bring new delights to Babar and his friends in Celesteville. ISBN 0-394-82882-8 [1. Seasons—
Fiction. 2. Elephants—Fiction] I. Title. II. Series: Just right book (New York, N.Y.) PZ7.B82843Babk 1989 [E]—dc19 88-35726
Manufactured in Singapore   1 2 3 4 5 6 7 8 9 0
JUST RIGHT BOOKS is a trademark of Random House, Inc.

It is a beautiful day in Celesteville. "Look!" cries Isabelle. "The leaves have turned red and yellow. And they are starting to fall."

"Yes," says Babar. "Autumn is here."

The air is cool and tingly now.
The older children play soccer.
Isabelle loves hopscotch. Does she see
the little squirrel who is gathering acorns?

For a special treat the children
visit a pumpkin patch.
Isabelle finds the biggest pumpkin of all.
Arthur will carry it home for her.

Pom has picked
a whole basket of apples.

Flora has picked corn.

Alexander has carved a pumpkin.
What a spooky face!

Winter has come to Celestevi
"Come play with us!"
the children shout to Cornelius.
"No, it is too cold for me,"
he tells them.

Cornelius prefers to read by the fire.
The Old Lady keeps him company.

For the holidays the whole family
goes to the mountains.
They enjoy skiing and sledding.
Look at all that snow!
It seems like winter will last forever.

But before you know it
spring is here.
The cherry trees have
burst into bloom.

Celesteville is full of beautiful flowers.
Arthur has picked some daffodils.

Zephir has picked some tulips.

Isabelle has found a nest of baby birds.

Babar loves to work in his garde
Flora and Pom help their father.

"Look, Mama! It's starting to rain,"
says Isabelle.
Celeste laughs.
"Now we won't need the hose
and watering can!"

The days turn sunny and warm.
Summer has come to Celesteville.
The children like to have picnics
by the lake.

After lunch the children play.
Isabelle has found a grasshopper.

Flora is trying to catch a butterfly.

"It's *so* hot," Pom says.
"I can't wait to go swimming!"

That's just what everyone does.
"Watch out below!" cries Alexander
as he jumps into the water.

Soon everyone must go home.
"I wish summer would last forever,"
says Arthur.